The FOOT BOOK

By

Dr. Seuss

RANDOM HOUSE NEW YORK

Published in the United States by Random House Children's Books,
a division of Random House, Inc., New York.

Random House and the colophon are registered trademarks of Random House, Inc.

Visit us on the Web!
www.randomhouse.com/kids
www.seussville.com
www.kohlscorporation.com

Educators and librarians, for a variety of teaching tools, visit us at
www.randomhouse.com/teachers

This special edition was printed for Kohl's by Random House Children's Books,
a division of Random House, Inc., New York.

ISBN: 978-0-375-86135-2

MANUFACTURED IN CHINA
10 9 8 7 6 5 4 3 2 1

Random House Children's Books supports the First Amendment and celebrates
the right to read.

Left foot
Left foot

Right foot
Right

Feet in the morning

Feet at night

Left foot

Left foot

Left foot

Right

Wet foot

Dry foot

High foot

Low foot

Front feet

Back feet

Red feet

Black feet

Left foot

Right foot

Feet

Feet

Feet

How many, many
feet you meet.

Slow feet

Quick feet

Trick feet

Sick feet

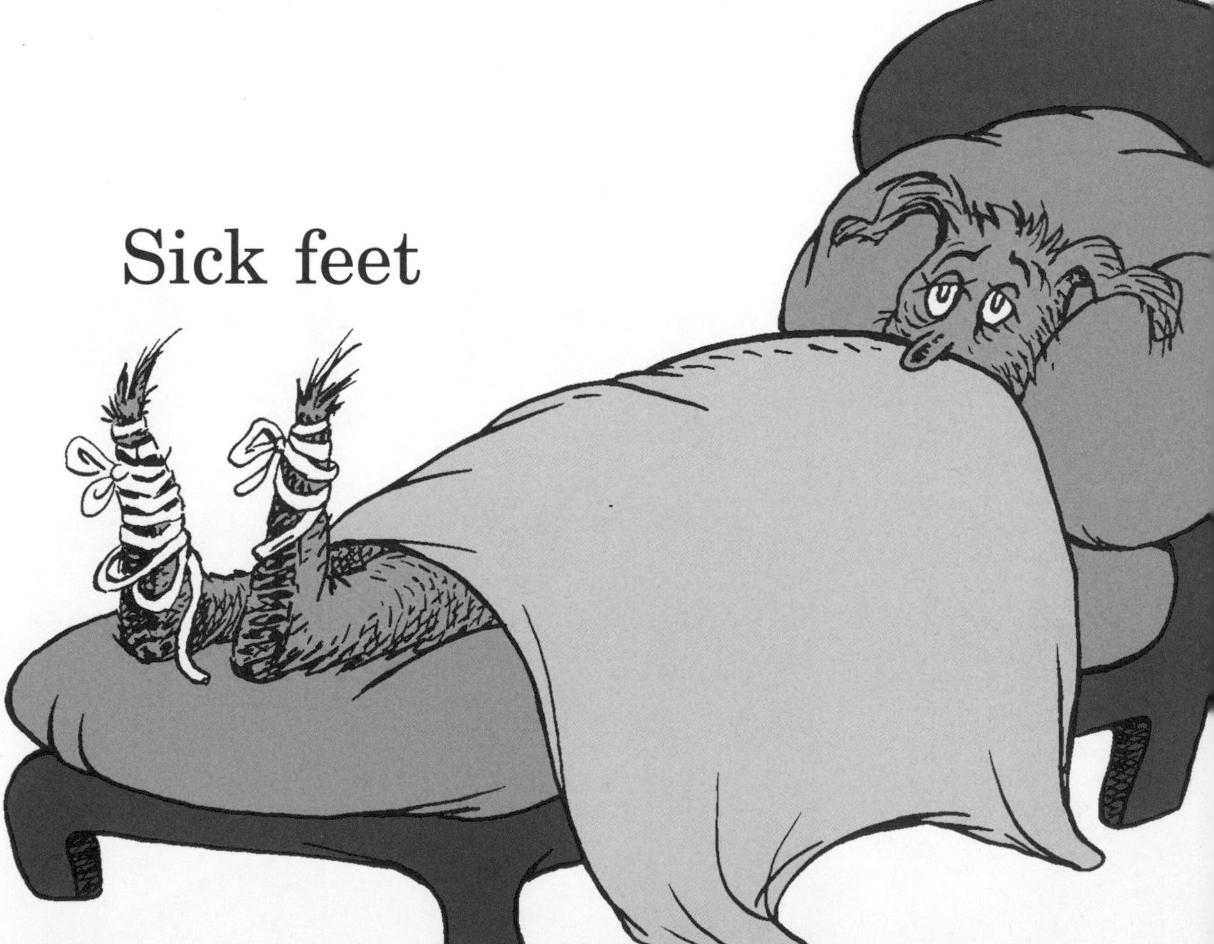

Up feet

Down feet

Here come clown feet.

Small feet

Big feet

Here come pig feet.

His feet

Her feet

Fuzzy fur feet

In the house,
and on the street,

how many, many
feet you meet.

Up in the air feet

Over a chair feet

More and more feet

Twenty-four feet

Here come
more and more . . . .

. . . . and **more** feet!

Left foot.

Right foot.

Feet. Feet. Feet.

Oh, how many
feet you meet!